ZERO EQUALS INFINITY

V YOGI

This book is a work of fiction. Names, characters, places, events and incidents either are the product of the author's imagination or are used fictitiously. Any resemblance to actual persons, living or dead, events, or locales is entirely coincidental.

ISBN: 978-0692868454

10 9 8 7 6 5 4 3 2 1

Printed in the United States of America

$$0 = \infty$$

PROLOGUE

A pin drop silence occurred, and all the students stood up as the math teacher entered the class. He waved his hand to nonverbally communicate that he accepted the respect and everyone could now sit down. He took a small piece of chalk and started writing on the blackboard.

'DIVISION' he wrote the heading on the board.

"For past couple of days, we are learning how to perform division," He said in an elevated voice to his third-grade kids. "Today we will learn a major rule in mathematics."

"Any number... Any number divided by itself is one."

"So, two divided by two is?"

"One?" A couple of kids sitting in the first row murmured.

"Absolutely right," the teacher said with a crooked smile.

"Three divided by three is?"

"One!" Half of the class shouted.

"Very good. Hundred divided by hundred is?"

"One!" This time, the whole class shouted.

“Sir, is Zero divided by Zero also one?” A voice came from the behind.

Now there was the same pin drop silence as before as everyone looked at the source of the voice. A skinny, tall kid with the gaze of the curiosity in his eyes was standing and looking at the teacher. He was *Advaita.*

The question brought some deep lines on the forehead of the teacher as in his career of twenty years no kid of his age ever asked him a question like this.

“You are too young to know that, Advaita.” he replied.

Everyone in the class burst into a huge laugh.

1

Advaita could not even wait to get out of the school so he could ask his most inquisitive question to his dad. “My dad will surely have an answer to this question. He knows everything.”

As he got home, he ran into his dad’s lap and asked, “Dad, today in the math class we were learning that any number divided by itself is one.”

“That’s right!”

“What is Zero divided by Zero?”

“Aren’t you too young for that?” Vedanta laughed.

“What? Math teacher said exactly the same thing.” Exclaimed Advaita.

“Why can’t I know, I am not too young, I am already seven now. Please please, tell me.”

Vedanta was having a hard time to think the way to explain his curious seven years old. He said, "Ok, how many times you can take two out of four?"

“Two times.” Advaita said without delaying for a second.

“And how many times you can take two out of two?"

“One.”

“And how many times you can take nothing out of nothing?”

The silence caught Advaita as it looked like he was scanning his whole mind for an answer.

“I don’t know.” He whispered.

“That's right,” Vedanta laughed and said. “The scientifically correct answer is Undefined.”

“What?”

“It means it is not possible, it can’t be defined, there is no assigned value.”

“What is not possible?”

“To divide 0 by 0.”

“You cannot take nothing out of nothing.”

For the first time, things were making sense to Advaita. But then suddenly he asked, “Can we take everything out of everything?”

Now the look on Vedanta’s face was remarkable. He could feel that his kid was not an ordinary human being and his eyes were almost begin to fill with the tears of proud, but he tried to stop them and said, “No, we can’t.”

He tried to think of his high school integral and differential calculus classes where he performed calculations of limit x tending to 0. He also remembered 0/0, ∞/∞ mentioned as "Undefined," but he never thought of it that time.

"We can't take everything out of everything." He answered.

"Dad, what they call Everything in mathematics?"

"INFINITY."

"It is called Infinity, Son."

It sounded like the best word ever heard to Advaita's ears. "Infinity." He tried to say exactly as his dad did. Vedanta took his ink pen out of his drawer and drew the symbol ∞ on his son's hand.

"So dad, it means Infinity contains everything, the sum of all the numbers?"

"Sort of!"

"What sort of?"Advaita looked at his dad with an eyebrow raised.

Vedanta took a pause, thought for a second and tried to remember the real, complex and non-standard analysis calculus he performed during his engineering and then said, "Yes."

"Would then Infinity contain Zero or not?" Advaita said.

Hearing those words from his seven years old kid, Vedanta was in a bigger shock than Advaita's math teacher.

Advaita continued, "How can everything contain

nothing?"

This time, Vedanta could not stop his tears of proud. He was almost hallucinating and seeing faces of Einstein, Newton, and Buddha in his son’s face.

Vedanta said, “That, I really don’t know. But I know that you will find your answer by yourself and solve this mystery."

2

Advaita's love and devotion for science and mathematics made him an Engineer. Keep solving all other problems at his job and at home, he was always wondering why he was doing this. All that amount of work? Why he wanted to know? To know more. To know more and more. To know everything. To know Infinity.

Why all those problems were arising which he was solving. If there were no problems, he would still probably be unemployed, unmarried. Why he was working so hard to solve problems outside him when he had a shit load of them in him.

He thought that he should have been a philosopher. The search for the source. The source of all. The source of his life, the source of all movement. The source of all the problems and solutions. He wanted to go away from all the problems and wander. Just wonder. He wanted to wonder why everything was the way it was.

He wanted to know the gravity. He wanted to know

Earth, Sun, the whole Universe.

He wanted to know why he was there. How everything came. And who was he? Why he existed? What was right, what was wrong? Where would he get all of those answers? He wanted to know the light. He always asked Sun. He was asking him all questions. And that one day when The Sun started answering.

He could feel the rays of the Sun transforming into his body and the perception of the light through his eyes was the process. His awareness being an observer was merging into the sight, the sight into the light and the light into Sun. He was completely absorbed in Sun. Then his mind dissolved with Sun's mind, and he was receiving the knowledge directly from Sun. He could see Earth rotating around himself and then the small Moon was rotating around her as a part of her. The gravitational waves emerging from him were making her rotating around him. She was looking so beautiful that he desired to look her closely. In the very next moment, his awareness got transferred to Moon. Then he started rotating and looking at her closely. The unconditional love was transforming into gravity. Then he desired to feel Earth physically as Sun and transmuted into the light falling directly on her skin.

Now for him, it was all Sunlight. All the forms coming in front of his eyes were various colors of

Sunlight. He saw it spreading into the seven colors and from those it was spreading into billions of colors. The engineer inside him connected this knowledge to his most favorite screen, his laptop screen. Where every pixel was either on or off, either there was light or no light. The black and white.

The depth of penetration of perception was getting deeper and deeper. He was able to differentiate specific forms, different permutations and combinations possible of the two aspects, light and dark. Taking various forms as different human beings, material objects, moving, unmoving. When the light was traveling at the unlimited speed, the knowledge was traveling at unlimited speed. And as it was perceived it started traveling at 299,792,458 meters per second. Now as the speed got slower, the perception went deeper, and it became denser. Because of seeing and having knowledge about a particular form and seeing several other variations, he was able to recognize that particular form and his intellect was able to discriminate that particular form from all the other forms he was seeing. The movement was creating the perception of life. The current of life was not only a movement, but it was also having its own gravity.

The white light was converting from monochromatic to high and true colors. And on the other side, it was dark. The light was changing forms, but the dark was changeless. Changeless as the deep sleep. The *Sushupti.* The waking life was changing every moment, the dreamer was perceiving the always changing dream state. But the Sushupti was changeless, motionless, timeless, eternal, bigger than the biggest and smaller than the smallest.

It was raining. He was experiencing the smell of the raindrops falling on the soil. His awareness of smell was merging in the smell of the rain and trees around him. After closing his eyes, he could hear the sound of drops, the water coming from the sky on Earth, as the collision of two particles created the sound. The drop was taking the form of whatever it fell on without judgment. It was merging in the soil, taking the form of the soil, merging in the pond, taking the form of the pond, and that drop which just fell on his face took the form of him.

And then he was that drop. That drop was him. He was watching infinite of other drops coming from the sky. And then disappearing as they fell on Earth, losing their current ego of a water drop and merging with the ego of Earth.

In the form of the light when he was falling on the water, he saw himself converting into the air and flying. Just flying, without any direction. He perceived his collision with other molecules as being another form of him, converting into the electricity. He was moving completely from one spark of electricity into the whole electric field of Earth.

Now he was losing awareness of the physical body as his sense awareness was peaking. He focused only on the sense of sight. The light was the observation, his sight was the process of the observation, and he was the observer. All the infinite forms of light, the appearance of trees, drops, the flying birds and his own body merged into one light. He could see the wave-particle duality. All he was perceiving was different forms of one light in wave form. And the process of observation was transforming the one wave into infinite particles. Each and every drop appeared as one separate particle. Once he moved his awareness on one drop on the green leaf, he saw that one drop was containing infinite particles of light. The drop slipped, the same wave of light which was falling on the drop now was falling on the green leaf.

The intensity of the light started increasing as the clouds were separating to reveal the divine view of Sun. It was the biggest source of light. Emitting enormous amount of energy in the form of light.

He could see himself outside of his body and be aware of the subtle world. Its subtle elements. He became the process of transformation of the observer into the object. The knowledge he could directly receive from Sun. By becoming it.

The whole picture of this sight was gone, and there was nothing, just darkness, as he closed his eyes. Again when he opened his eyes, everything appeared again. Only after realizing the true form of light, he could experience the duality of the light and dark in his every blink.

The duality of nature was in front of him, light to no light and no light to light, in every blink. From the presence of light to the absence of light. He was the perceiver, he was perceiving both light and dark. He was beyond the duality, the duality of nature.

The light was as true as the dark. They were existing in a pair. The light was always following the dark and dark was always following the light. On a denser physical level, Earth's very rotation was creating the same duality. The day and night. Only the length of presence and absence of light was creating a different experience of time whether it was a second or 12 hours. The two dimensional Sun became three dimensional, and he could see the space beyond Sun. Sun's light was creating the light sphere around it. He saw the other side of Earth's orbit around Sun, where he would be in 6 months.

He thought about the view of Earth from Sun. He thought of traveling to Sun to see Earth from there. Suddenly his sight got attached to Sun. His awareness started traveling through his eyes on the wave of light. The same wave of light which was coming from Sun was reflecting in his eyes and was taking his awareness back to Sun. He could feel the wave of light coming in his eyes, converting into sight perception and traveling to his brain through neurons. He could feel Sun in the center of his brain. The wave of light was connecting the center of his brain to the center of Sun. And he could see himself as the reflection. His awareness merged into Sun's awareness. As the Sun, he was physically experiencing the body of Earth through its Sunlight. And enjoying the sight of her through zillions of eyes of living beings, every moment. He was touching her through his heat. It was all light. No dark. No duality.

But how was that possible. There had to be dark for light to exist. To know that he needed to go beyond the Sun and expand his awareness beyond the Solar system.

What was after the Sun. The light traveling from the Sun, ending at some point and then there was dark. Sun was knowledge, darkness was ignorance. Knowledge was a flash, ignorance was always there. No beginning, no end. Pure ignorance. The knowledge was changing, taking various forms, science, religion, art, mathematics, yoga, music, and whatever perceivable but the ignorance was changeless. The knowledge was coming from the ignorance and again was dissolving in it. Sun was burning himself to keep the ignorance away.

He went beyond the Sun's light sphere, and there he found the duality, the dark. As a piece of matter, Sun also had physical limits, and its light also had limits. It could travel at a certain speed of c. The sunlight was also not permanent. In a few million years, the Sun, the fireball, which was producing an immense amount of light and heat due to the weak nuclear force converting Sun's body mass into energy, would fade away. It would burn all of its mass and then convert into a black hole. It would die. The whole solar system would die. There would be darkness. All the events and things he experienced in his life were so tiny compared to what Sun would experience. Ultimately there would be the end of Sun.

The Sun was small. The Earth was big. He couldn't control her. He needed *Mahima.* Through Mahima he had to suck up everything and hold it at *Manipura* to become fire and go back to the Sun, leaving the Earth. Against her gravity. When trillions of other neutrinos like him were falling on Earth and becoming her. He needed to go back to Sun. The pain to leave Earth. The attachment to Earth. The pain was separation. The desire to go up. To sublime. To be converted directly into Light from Earth. Skipping the process of melting it to water. That was sublimation. Directly from solid to vapor. Earth element transmuting into Air element.

He was invisible. Invisible to Earth. Journey to the Sun. Many of him tried in the form of water but became cloud, enjoyed the sky and came back to Earth. They were not able to defy her gravity. He needed *Laghima.* To become light. So he could travel wherever he wanted against the will of Earth. He wanted to be free of gravity, free of Earth. There was an intense pain to leave Earth and fly. Fly wherever he wanted, without attachment of Earth. In his body, he could walk, run wherever he wanted, but the speed was limited. He wanted to travel faster. The pain was received. The liberation was received. Liberation from the mass, liberation from the weight. He was lighter. He was light. He was Sun.

3

The tremendous amount of energy was being generated from the Sun. Where was it getting all this energy from? This all was coming from the very center of the Sun. The heat and light were being generated from the center of the Sun. The center of the Sun was the purest form of *Sattva guna* in the manifested universe.

Two forces were interplaying together. Centripetal and centrifugal force. That was his love of life, which was causing fear of death. He wanted to survive, not losing his current form, current ego, current definition, current body, current moment, each and every second. The fear was rooted in *Mooladhara*, the root of his spine, the attachment to Earth, to earth element. The gravity of Earth was so powerful, it was keeping him rooted in her, attached. But he could see that on Earth it was less degree of freedom. He could see the sky and wanted to be air, free of weight, free from the gravity of Earth, free from all of her forms. How would that be possible? Even his body was Earth. The weight his pranic body was carrying, borrowed from Earth. Earth gave a degree of freedom, to roam around over her. If he wanted to jump, the very next moment she was pulling him back. The interaction of Earth and Sun was creating the various visual forms of Earth.

One morning, when he was just about to wake up, one of his sense awareness was coming back on the physical plane first. It was hearing. He started listening. Listening to the sound. The sound as a whole. Different voices, including the sound of his breath, or the sound of his wife talking on the phone, or the subtle sound he just experienced in one of his dreams. All was one sound wave coming to his ear, going to mind, getting discriminated in various categories by his intellect, recognizing the source of the sound, deriving the meaning and producing the live experience of sound element.

The sound he was listening, was the cause of the sound he was able to create through his speech. One of his organs of actions. Through the learned movement of his body parts to produce various forms of sound. Providing them a shape, in the form of knowledge, music, singing. But that was not him, who was producing the sound. Just the music was being produced. That was music's desire for being produced and it just was coming. Then going out of him. In outer space, going to the other room, to the next floor but then what? Then just disappearing. Disappearing into the space. Where it came from. Like it was never there. Just the knowledge of having it a live experience was there. And then there was a desire to create it again. He watched this wave, being born, sustained and then annihilated. Then his mind performed his favorite task of shaping this wave, taking the form of the words, creating the meaning. For what?

To communicate. To communicate with the awareness outside of his physical body. To call his wife because he wanted the morning tea, his daily after waking up rituals and some fire plays. He didn't know what happened, but then this desire took the form of a sound wave, words, he called her.

The reality completely got changed as she came in the bedroom. The another form of life beside him in the closed apartment. Extension of his ego. Its female form. What was he thinking before that he could choose what to speak, which thought he wanted to convert into the speech he could. Now the limit of that ego, that identity, got decreased. Now he would only speak what would be pleasing to her.

The sound was matter, the hearing was antimatter. Awareness attached to the matter. The combination of different frequencies of the sound was creating a wave, taking the form of words, as the light was taking the electric and magnetic form. This knowledge of sound in the form of the words was working behind his ability to understand these different frequencies encoded in the words. The same sound wave he was producing every time he was speaking. What an amazing ability humanity had developed, language, the control over this piece of matter in the mouth, the breath, and the will to produce it. That was just on a micro level happening in his subconscious, one of other millions of calculations his intellect performed to provide him the knowledge behind that sound.

He just needed to direct his awareness towards the sound to receive knowledge of it. The words were traveling through sound as the light traveled in the electricity. The words could use another means and could travel through the light. The source of the recognition of different sound was lying in his knowledge of the different sources of the sound he experienced in his past. He could recognize the voice, and once he had the knowledge of words, he understood the meaning. By understanding the connection between the source of the sound and the meaning, he could understand the feeling behind it. His physical body was just present there. His mental body made of the subtle senses was working. His mental body received the sound, presented in front of the intellect. The intellect separated the words from the sound and looked for the meaning, and came up with the feeling in front of his causal body. That was him right now. The pain. If moments ago, she said something else, some other words, may be words of appreciation, the feeling would be opposite of this one which he was experiencing now.

The sound was being produced by another human body. The same human ego which was in him was outside of him too. The sound was carrying the thought, as food carried the taste. That was how their minds were communicating. The thought, the subtle energy, the subtle modification of mind was happening in two different individual minds, and interchange was happening from the speech.

The center of both ears. The sound coming in from his two different gross ears, merging into one and providing him the live experience of hearing.

He was paying attention to all the sounds which were coming to him. The sound of the running water, the sound of the wind, the sound of the birds, so many other sounds which were absent to him before. Then he closed his ears with his fingers and started listening to the sound inside of him. They were so many, he could differentiate, from low to high frequencies, sounding like birds, bees, insects. Which were these sounds? As his perception of sound got deeper, he was able to differentiate frequencies and vibration of the sound waves. And then suddenly there was his favorite.

The silence. The silence was so soothing, so calm, so blissful. All the other sound were changing, coming and going, but the silence was always same, changeless, formless, dimensionless.

It was a tough task for him to travel at the speed of sound, at the speed of the physical object to manifest it, instead of traveling at the speed of light, at the speed of thought, which was more Vivacious. To travel as a cloud and have more degree of freedom than traveling at the speed of the water drop. The sky element was dominating in him. The clouds in the sky, transforming in the drops, the thoughts manifesting in the sound and words.

He thought that when silence was unchanging and nondifferentiable, why not sound. Then it was there. The magical moment. Where he heard the cosmic sound. That sound was one. All that his ears were able to perceive were infinite forms of one sound. Some forms were louder, some were softer, arising from random sources and then merging into silence. Then other forms emerging, never ending sound, beginningless sound. Only its form had beginning and end. The boundaries. When all was perceived without judgment facility, the intellect. There was no perception of differentiation. As the perception happened and he moved his awareness to a particular wavelength of the sound, the wave collapsed and manifested into sound which was again perceived by his mind and then his intellect provided the meaning associated with it.

But there were still two. Sound and silence. Were they two?

Everything was coming out of that silence. The words were flying and ready to obey him. They lost their gravity and completely surrendered to him. He was waving the fingers, and the words were following him. Beyond the reach of Earth's gravity. Piercing through matter. The unknown's gravity was beyond the limits of the intellect, the known. The sky was becoming dark. The silence became the light. The water was the body, and the breath was a denser form of mind. The sound was Sun, Earth was water. Shit was everywhere inside and outside. Gold was everywhere, inside and outside. Food was everywhere. Sex was everywhere. Male was everywhere. Female was everywhere. Atom was everywhere. Light was everywhere. Dark was everywhere. Everything was meaningless. Everything was meaningful. Smoke everywhere. Thoughts everywhere. Faces everywhere.

Forms everywhere. Knowledge everywhere. Ignorance everywhere. White everywhere. Black everywhere. Virtue everywhere. Sin everywhere. Fragrance everywhere. Stink everywhere. Nectar everywhere. Poison everywhere. Trust everywhere. Cheat everywhere. Everything was manifesting from negative to positive Infinity, combining with Zero in each and every pixel. She was *Prakriti.*

4

The words were getting assigned an immediate value between negative to positive Infinity. Everything was weightless. The weight was free to be assigned. The particle was carrying the weight. The wave was weightless. Light was weightless. Air was weightless. Earth was weightless. Weight was flying. Without gravity. With gravity.

Sight was light. Touch was smell. Tongue was feet. Religion was belief. Science was religion. Left was auspicious, right was sinister.

The speech. The speech was the cause of pain. Pain transmitting through the words and the tone. The poison through the needle. The same speech was the kiss of nectar. It was oscillating between sound and silence. Some sound was known, some was unknown. Silence was always unknown. The sound was taking the form of honey and the arrow. From silence, anything could have arisen. Suddenly. Without warning. Out of nothing.

And when he was silent, she was using all of her power to make him speak. But he was silent. Sometimes requesting, sometimes ordering, sometimes crying, sometimes torturing. All was present to him so he could manifest, he could create, and she loved his expressions. She knew all were his various forms. Whether he was angry or jealous. Whether he was in pain or pleasure. But then something became aware of itself, identity took the form of ego, and she chose. She wanted him to experience pleasure not pain.

Speech was the problem. Silence was the solution. Light was the problem, dark was the solution. Light was piercing dark and sound was penetrating into silence.

Speech was the expression. Tongue was its work organ. The dancing piece of meat was aware of itself. Choosing on itself which thought to manifest. The control over the movement of it was *Samyama.* Samyama on speech. Samyama on *Vishuddha.* Samyama in Space. Samyama in Sound.

Now his awareness went to the subtle sound. The sound which he would experience while reading. Each and every word his eyes were reading was resonating in his subtle sense of hearing. And he was listening, listening to his own voice, resonating in his mind, and creating the experience of reading. The sound was hiding somewhere in the black inked paper.

All of his other senses were free to roam around. But they weren't. They were shut. The whole voltage of awareness was going to the eyes. The sight. They were acting. Their vision was creating the subtle sound, resonating in his mind. It was creating a completely different universe, for him, to experience. The universe which he could not show to anyone else. The touch and smell were engaged in the feel of the book and fragrance of papers. His morning tea was completing engagement of his five senses.

The will, which was separate from the flesh body yet the part of it. It was controlling the flesh. The will was formless, taking the shape of the body. There was a will to eat. He was moving his hands to pick up the food to eat. His mind was creating the body. The mind was subtle, the body was gross. The will was creating the mind. The will was his power. His equality but still not him. The mind was subtle. Very subtle. Formless. And the same mind was taking the form of the gross body.

Thought was subtle. Speech was gross. Thought was incoming. Speech was outgoing. Speed of thought was trillions times faster than speed of speech. Thought was unmanifested, speech was manifested.

Speech was action of his gross body. Thought was action of his subtle body.

What was connecting these two? That was *Prana.* As it was connecting the mental body to physical body. The outgoing breath was his tool to produce the work of speech. Physical breath was producing the sound. The subtle, the prana was separate from it.

The breath was physical, incoming and outgoing air. The air was just carrier. The atoms of oxygen were just carrier. It was carrying Prana. It was so subtle. It was the first time he was able to perceive prana and breath separately. He perceived breath carrying prana as wire carrying the electricity. The prana was carrying the mind.

The awareness went back into his physical body, and he started observing his physical self. He was breathing. Slowly. He watched his breath entering from the nose and going inside his nose. And then coming back. He came to know that his breath was connecting his body and his mind.

He wondered. "What is there between my breaths?"

"How the chain of the breath is getting connected?"

He started flowing with his breath. The chain of the breath was the current of his awareness. The cognition of smell suddenly increased. He could perceive that his sense of smell was creating the perception of the earth element. Then it started moving in his mouth, and then it concentrated on his tongue. He then could feel that the sense of taste was creating the perception of the water element. Then, the current of the consciousness spread into the eyes, and he could clearly see his eyes creating the perception of light. In the very next moment, it spread all over his body, covering all the skin, and he could feel the touch. The touch of air. He knew that his skin was creating the perception of touch. And then he paid his full attention to the sound coming in his ears. The ears were creating the perception of the sound.

His body was made of the same elements which he perceived outside. Then he started wondering, "Is perception of my senses creating the outside world or because of the outside world the senses exist?"

Then he realized that the body parts nose, tongue, eyes, skin, and ears were gross elements, made of Earth. The actual perception was very subtle. His whole awareness went to very subtle level, and he could perceive his subtle body, within the physical body, yet separated. The subtle body had very subtle elements. He was perceiving the subtle elements of smell, taste, sight, touch and hearing separated from his respective physical body parts. He was floating in the subtle plane of existence. He wondered, "Are they exactly same subtle senses through which I perceive my dream world?"

As he was paying attention to his subtle sense of smell. He felt his subtle body was not limited to his physical body. The sensory perception of smell was reaching well distance outside of him. Exactly same with his all other sensory perceptions. He was the observer, and nature was the observation.

"Are these subtle senses combined as my mind?" He thought.

"No. These subtle elements are perceived by the mind. So the mind is the observer. What happens in imagination, when I am thinking? I can still experience my thoughts whether in the past or future. So my subtle body is not limited by time. Well, then it is not limited by space either."

He now could see that he was recognizing the other human bodies by their appearances, their egos which were created in his mind by the past memory of his experiences with them, their expressions through their work organs.

The eyes, the light were taking various forms, he was entering into another beings by their sense of sight. The light was falling on him, and he was absorbing all the colors except the perception of his physical body. The words he was speaking, were taking a form of sound and coming out of him and entering other ears, the fragrance he was wearing, was his smell, the taste could take the vehicle of his bodily fluid or the food cooked by him, his touch was completing the control of five senses.

The past became the part of nature. Every second things which were in his control were converting into unchangeable past. The future was also the part of nature, there could infinite things happen which were beyond his control. He was dependent on Earth every second to create oxygen, on Sun to produce light, on Water, on food. To sustain, to survive physically.

The water. He was contemplating on the water in the glass in front of him. The water in the glass was outside him. But as he drank it became him. It was inside him. Physical him. And it went outside also. The body was eliminating it. It was a process. An ongoing process. What was happening to the water? It was there outside, and now it was inside. The same water. Just the container changed. From the glass to a physical body. And its form would also change due to the chemical reactions in the body. He was water. Whether it was inside or outside. The thought brought the same water from his eyes. He was watching himself flowing outside his own eyes.

The ego of water was changing according to the temperature outside. At 100 C it was becoming so pure, it was unstable and changing the form. Vapor, more degree of freedom, freedom of movement. When the temperature dropped, it became dense, more physical, less movement, the polarity of the vapor. As stuck with the chain of beliefs, created denseness. His densest belief was his name. A random combination of sounds and letters given by his dad became his name. He was recognized by that sound. Other beliefs were changing frequently, as the surroundings changed. The name was given to the ego. Son of Dad.

At the same time, he could hear the bird, the bird flying around and making a sound. For him, it was just sound. The sound traveling. The source of the sound was also traveling. The body of the bird was made of the same flesh, the same earth, the same water, and the same will. Which was encased in the other body. Producing the sound. The sound was produced by the will. The air inside the bird's body was colliding with the windpipe in its throat and creating the sound. The will was making the movement of the air. And then energy changing form and converting into the sound. How the will was moving the air. He came back to his body and produced the sound. He was producing the sound. The same way. The will was producing the sound. Or the sound was getting produced? By what? The particles of the air were colliding with particles of his body. It was the conversion of the energy. The same way he moved his hand and the static energy was getting converted into kinetic energy.

Ego made up of what he was, how respected he was, how accomplished he was, what were his possessions, his family, his friends, and everything associated with him. And the densest layer of ego was his physical body.

He saw his causal body in pain, the similar physical pain he could experience, would be the pain when he almost broke his hand when he slipped on the icy pathway and fell down. If he didn't go to check out the gas station, he would have skipped the slip, that blow of nature.

He could still feel the presence of that pain. Which was bigger. The very next moment when he watched from his causal body, how much he was attached to see the picture of the house on his laptop screen. Only the thought of living there while watching those pictures was a pleasure. Might be better than the reality would be. The duality was present there also, but he experienced it moments later when he knew he could not just be there physically, in that world, pulling away his attention from there, was a pain. He needed to get over it, come out of that maze created by his own mind. He was only able to perceive either pain or pleasure at one point. To perceive the duality he needed to go to the other point.

The existence had polarities. And it was existing because of the identification. The nothing, the Zero didn't have polarities because it was not identifiable. Once the identification happened, it created, and it always existed in dualities. If there were two, there was space between those two. To define the movement, one had to be fixed or to be taken as the point of reference. If there were just two points, it was impossible to know which one was moving. For one point it was always the other, which was moving. She was *Relativity*.

5

He was watching his thoughts. Very carefully. Minutely. One by one. Thought by thought. One thought came. Then it went. Then another came. Then it went. And then for some time, there was no thought.

Now he realized the movement of mind. The thought was a mere movement of mind. The modifications of mind were producing the thoughts. His subtle senses. The mind was expressing itself through subtle senses, and these were thoughts.

"What would happen after I leave this body?" He thought.

"After the death?"

Was there any way for him to know?

For that, he needed to know what his body was. He Moved his attention to his physical body.

Depression took over his face with this thought. "Death is the only reality." He thought, "Which is unchangeable and certain." All other things were just forms, coming and going. Born, lived, died. Creation, sustaining, destruction. Painful thoughts. One moment ago he was experiencing the heaven, and now he started experiencing the hell at the very same place.

"One day, I will die, this body will be no more, the family will be no more, whatever I have done or earned will be no more, this world will be no more, this universe will be no more. everything is temporary."

Then, his mind became silent. Totally silent. Sadness was taking over his before happy face. Was that the fear of death?

The boss of all. He was *Abhinivesha*. To kill him, he needed to kill the desire to live too. The desire deeply rooted in every living being. His body was breathing, his heart was beating for the desire to live. The desire for the existence to be as it was. How would anyone come over that? The only way was knowledge of him.

The only and ultimate certainty was death. Death of everyone, everything, earth, sun, universe, every atom of the universe. It needed to exist because of life. The life was transforming into death as the blink of an eye. In every blink, there was another pulse of the awareness. If the blink was longer, the reality outside him would have changed, perhaps from night to day, dark to light. When he looked at his past, it felt like a blink. Who was the one, living all these moments. Not him, because he was there, right now. Right there. Still hanging out in his crib, sitting in the same posture for so long. Suddenly the past disappeared and his mind became silent.

"The only certainty is death." the thought just got stuck in his mind and kept resonating, increasing his pain and grief continuously. How would he overcome this depressing thought and why was this thought causing him pain?

He realized that this was his attachment to the life, the survival instinct, the very basic instinct. Instinct, which was deeply rooted in his mind. The hunger, the thirst were getting triggered by this instinct.

Was this attachment, this instinct only for his life? There were other forms of human life too. His family, his friends, his enemies. The knowledge of the end of any of his loved lives would bring him grief. Even after realizing that these all were various temporary forms taken by Earth, he was deeply attached to these forms of awareness, and he wanted them to remain.

"Why? Why I am so attached to these all forms?" He thought. "Why I am so fearful when I have a thought of losing my possessions?"

He now was experiencing the duality of life and death. The only way to come over the fear of death was to go beyond the life too. Leaving the attachment to the life.

He stopped at those moments, one after another, some were giving him pleasure, some were giving him pain. Highs and Lows of pain and pleasure. He had no control over them. He tried so hard, prayed them to stop, surrendered, but they did not stop.

At that extremity, his intellect pierced his ego, and it merged with the outer, as the air within the bubble merged with outside after it burst. Before that, the bubble was wanting to increase its size, as the entropy of closed system was always increasing. It was traveling at the speed of the wind around him, but now it started traveling at the speed of the air, at the speed of the sound, then the speed of the light. The speed of light? Why not more? What was the layer of the ego? The layer of the ego of the light? If that was the layer he had reached, he had reached the maximum speed a particle, matter could travel through. What sense he could use as the tool? The light was perceived by his sense of sight, he could not perceive it by his sight. All it could perceive was light.

The resistance which was decreasing the speed of his travel was his own intellect. His intellect discriminating the one from many, the depth of perception, was determined by how much prior knowledge was there being used to perform the discrimination. The decision making identity, which way to go, right or left.

He wanted to measure. The intensity of good and bad. He needed numbers. He needed scales. He came to know about the evolution of the number system. The desire to measure. The desire to measure the separation. Separation from Infinity. The Infinity had everything in it. It was existing in duality. The negative and positive. The negative scale was subtle, not physical. The mirror image of positive. As the magnetic field was creating positive and negative simultaneously. He thought he would not enjoy the negative. So he broke the magnet to get rid of the negative.

But then what? Now that positive half created positive and negative within itself. The same happened with the negative half. He now knew it could not happen for only positive to exist. Only good happening, only love, not possible.

The will was making his prana to push more. Put more pressure on the scale. Something invisible in him was increasing the weight. The Force. That was his prana. That force was invisible. The prana was invisible yet combined with matter, with his body, bending the space-time fabric. Which was coming and going, continuously through breath, through air, in every living being. It was the prana, making Sun rotate and travel. As his prana was making his body move. Every time he wanted to lift his end. His will to move his hand was moving prana, and the prana was moving his body. The prana was causing the movement in all living beings. Invisible, yet moving the matter. Controlling the matter. Manipulating the matter and its gravity. The universal prana permeating in the whole universe. He was *Dark matter.*

The Sun was rotating because of prana. It was breathing. As he was inhaling and exhaling, which was making his belly move. The Sun was rotating on its axis to breathe. The Earth was rotating to breathe. The Moon was rotating to breathe. All stars were rotating to breathe.

The prana was very subtle. Subtler than matter, molecules, atoms, subatomic particles, quarks. What was subtler than the prana. He thought. He moved his attention to his hand. His hand movement. The prana was moving his hand. What was moving the prana, inside his body? It was moving automatically. The magic machine. The human body. The breath was automatic.

His thought. He had a thought. To move his hand. And prana followed the thought. It was so fast. So so fast. So so subtle. The mind. The mind was subtler than the prana. The mind was perceiving. His intellect had a will to move the hand. Intellect made the judgment, to move the hand. And then his mind which was governing the flow of prana. The thought in his mind was the reason for that specific movement of prana to move his hand. The thought which came to his mind. The thought to move the hand. The mind. The mind was subtler than the prana. The universal mind permeating in the whole universe. She was *Dark energy.*

The body's prana was able to communicate with another prana by physical contact. As his hand was picking up the glass of water. *Vyana* of hand was moving the hand. This move was initiated by the thirst, and the body knew what it needed to do to satisfy that. The instinct was moving the prana. As thirst was being born from the survival instinct.

The prana was oscillating between *Ida* and *Pingala.* In the middle there was *Sushumna.* The left was Ida, the Moon. The Right was Pingala, the Sun.

His will to move overcame Earth's will to not letting him move. Vyana of his legs was making the physical feet move. To wander. And it was outside him everywhere, in other beings. Was this will free?

He thought so, so he ran, he slowed down. He had limitations. He always wanted to run faster. And faster. He couldn't. If it was free will, he could fly, wherever he wanted, with any speed he would desire. He was still the piece of Earth. Earth's gravity was overtaking his, after some time. After some time he had to completely relax, completely lose himself and let his body surrender to Earth. He remembered that it was not his prana, it was borrowed from Earth's prana. It was Earth's prana.

The will was connected to the prana. To move any part of his body, he was requesting prana to move in that part of the body. He had received the knowledge from his past to move his body, to walk, to dance, to move his fingers on his guitar, on his laptop, on his phone. The muscles had their own memory, and it was connected to Vyana. Vyana was coming from the prana. The prana was traveling on his breath, as electricity in the wire, as heat in the light. The prana was the moving Force. It was moving the piece of Earth. That prana was able to move outside prana also, as the smoke was coming out of his mouth and going wherever it wanted during his Hatha yoga. The desire overcame the intellect to bring the masochist inside him.

In the form of light. Each and every particle of light was carrying the awareness of the whole Sun, all the knowledge of the Sun. Its all colors, wavelength, carried by his quanta. He was the source of the light. Earth was rotating around him. That was true love, true devotion of Earth towards Sun. They were in their perfect geometry. The gravity was not just because of the physical weight, a piece of mass. It was the will of the Sun and the will of the Earth, their prana, and their mind. Their understanding together. Sometimes if she was getting mad, she was trying to go away, Sun was pulling her back. She was going back as she could not bear too much of his *Tejas.* That would burn her.

Earth was breathing. He could feel when he just surrendered to her. And then both breaths synchronized. His mind stopped, and then he was Earth again.

6

He was running away from pain. Running towards the pleasure. He was running away from the sources which were giving him pain, towards the sources which would provide him pleasure. Where was the pain? Where was the pleasure? The source of pleasure was gone, then its absence was becoming the source of the pain.

The pain was the cry. The pleasure was the laugh. The pain was bad, and pleasure was good. He was trying to find the causes. Why? Why he even needed to face pain? Could not it be just pleasure?

The pleasure was the desire. To evolve. The desire got bigger, better, stronger. When the mind saw or thought of something, and judged on the scale of feeling, it wanted. It wanted that something. The source of pleasure. The possible extension of him, of his body, of his ego which would make him bigger than what he was now. The mind was stuck there. It was now pulling his body there, to merge with the perceivable source of pleasure.

The pain was his inability to merge with that source. When the cosmos was not letting him collapse into the source of pleasure. That was *Cosmological constant.* The pain was dark. The mind was pain. The pain was real. The pleasure was imaginary. The seek for the pleasure was more beautiful, more intriguing, more lustful than the pleasure itself. The appearance of pain was scarier than the pain itself.

As the desired pleasure was achieved, there was guilty. The desire of pleasure was more vivid than the pleasure itself. The pain within the pleasure. The video game he loved in his childhood, he was working hard every time just to finish it, complete it and the day he did, the attachment was gone. He was free of that game. The pleasure was then vanished. What he achieved and what he lost, canceled out and then there was Void. The absence of desire. He came to rest. The cosmos came to rest. All the kinetic energy converted into the static, and the object was at rest until an outside force came to move it.

When he was experiencing the heaven, his duality was experiencing the hell. Just the knowledge of the pain in the other was building guilty in him. Guilty of enjoying the heavenly experience when his complementary was experiencing the hell.

He did not want to experience that pain either. He

wanted just pleasure. Only that was the desire. And he did not want to cause pain to the counterpart. The desire of the pleasure was causing the pain. And then pain was causing more pain having revenge as the catalyst. The uncontrolled reaction was taking place, and the survival instinct was ordering him to fight or flight. If he fought, it would cause massive destruction. His ordinary Astra was more deadly than the Brahmastra. It could cause complete destruction. The fire could burn all the trees. So he had to choose flight.

The pleasure was coming to him through those fingers. When he was sucking his thumb, picking the skin carefully, so there was no small piece of skin sticking out. Manicuring with teeth. What was so juicy, so tasty about that. For others, it was so disgusting. The pain was coming later. The reaction of this masochism, when he was washing dishes, he was realizing how cruelly he bit them. Those poor fingers. They were in Hell. Suffering, without any of their faults.

This brought an intensive feeling of guilt in him, not just because of that pain he was habitual of since his childhood, but the thought, every pleasure he was receiving, was creating pain in another form. To other forms including his own ego.

It was all inside him, he was looking for the source of pleasure, and pain, outside. But it was coming from him. The source was inside and seemed to be arising from nowhere, because it was arising from nowhere, the *Shunya.*

That headache, suddenly arising. From nowhere. It was not there a moment ago. And now it was there. He would have guessed so many reasons where it came from.

The pain and the pleasure were getting created simultaneously, their appearances were different, as he experienced pleasure, the pain was the absence of that pleasure. As the pleasure was becoming more intoxicating, the absence of it was stretching limits of the pain associated with that pleasure.

He wondered what was the pleasure behind biting the nails, cutting the piece of his own body, sucking it and spitting it away. Why he was biting his own skin away, what kind of masochism was this? The pain was coming later when the fingers touched the hot water. He wished he would not have done that.

The pain was attached to the incidents, the memory was always making it difficult to take the incidents apart from the pain. If those bizarre moments did not happen, he would not have experienced the various frequencies of pain. But then he realized that the pain was making him better from what was he before experiencing it, his ego was stretched.

But how much it would stretch, what would be the limit of his intellect, his ego, that would be stretched to the maximum and what would happen after that? It would burst, then it would convert into a Black hole. He was *Black hole.* The peace, the absence, the Zero. In its pure absence. No relativity as there was no one to perceive, nothing to perceive, no duality, no space, no time, just pure absence. As he was never there.

When it was all right. Everything was fine. Still, there was pain. The memory of pain. Some incidents were so severe that the memory of them was so fresh. He could feel the scars hurting. The suffering body was getting the *Yatana.* It was being tortured, and he was feeling this pain, there was the reaction in his present body. Why he was remembering all the pain which was not there now. It was past. Gone. Why those moments, those experiences always coming back to him and grilling him. Where he could just feel guilty. Guilty of not being good. Not being perfect. Guilty of the inferior actions performed where he could have thought of a better solution, better word, better argument, better slap, better punch or more deadly venom.

That was all in vain. Those moments, people, situations were gone. Why they were still bugging him. It had been several times, he thought about those, got rid of, they were still haunting him.

How could he be perfect? How could he be happy by himself? He would be happy if he saw others happy. So to make himself happy, he was disappearing their pain. What he knew less that the happiness of providing help, would bring more pain. He could only be at one place, concentrating on one event, one situation, one action, one person, one entity. But there were many, at the same time. He was being accused of not solving other problems, the other people, he did not get a chance to reach to. And the problems was never ending for the same source. They were coming up with all of their problems. Now they knew he could solve their problem, save them from pain.

But it was tough for him, he was human, he had limitations like every other human. But they were not able to see this. They did not want to care about this. All they cared about their pain. And he knew he would fail, the problems were dark, unknown. Some would take a lot of time. Still, the blame would come, blame for being late, not giving his best, and not caring enough.

Was that all good work for? For being blamed?

Finding flaws was very easy even in the most perfect solution. Some eyes were only finding flaws. He hated them. He wanted to show them the mirror and their ugly faces so they could work on their own imperfections, not his.

All those cacophonous voices, painful voices. He wanted them to shut up. He wanted to remove and destroy the root of that *Tamas*.

There would be guilty. Guilty of punishing his owns. The other way was flight. Walk away. That was easy, to walk away. The solution of the problems. The happiness was just a flash. It occurred and went away within the fraction of a second. Now again there was guilty. He escaped with physical body but left the suffering body in that Hell. It was connected. It was getting punished. He was getting punished. Blamed, guilty. He would never be able to experience that live, what notorious nouns would be getting attached to his name, his identity. He wanted to go back and tell it was wrong. He was right, and he wanted to fight for it.

The extreme happiness and agony were sharing the expression in the form of tears. The same human reaction in the extremities of pleasure and pain.

He could feel the needle of an intense headache. The pain of facing Tamas guna. The gravity, the repulsion of the Tamas guna, in the eyes of that person. The male duality. They both were feeling pain and repelling in the form of the unconscious facial expressions and the tone of speech. The repulsion of positive and positive. The egos created bigger boundaries around themselves and wanted to claim more of their space.

As much as he tried to achieve Sattva guna, Tamas was manifesting suddenly with greater intensity. In the form of hate, jealousy, and numerous other forms. The other was hating him out of jealousy. Being mad at him for being complete while he was not. He wanted to steal, snatch whatever he had if he was not able to get alike. Being Sattva was painful. Being hated, being guilty, when he was innocent. Wishing good even for Tamas. Not cursing him in the hope that it would change. Pure hearted, pure gold. He was not stable. The pure gold was not stable. He was losing form even with a tiny collision, a tiny blow. The Earth was not the place for the gold. He wanted to leave Earth. It was painful being pure gold. He needed Tamas. A drop of Tamas, the poison was his need. He needed to be impure so he could live on the earth plane. To fight Tamas, the dark, the bad, the ugly, the stinky. When Tamas saw Sattva's poison, he was afraid. Now the before appearing harmless Sattva was not harmless anymore. He had poison, he had Snake. He had the ability to kill the poison, to kill Tamas.

The more he knew about the Tamas, the less accurate his prediction of the presence and the movement of Tamas was. She was *Uncertainty.* All forms were deceiving. Tamas was disguised. In the forms of Sattva.

This time Tamas was Her.

Her poison was appearing nectar. Her cacophony was sweet. She was burning him. She was Tamas only for him. For others, she was innocent, pure. But only he could see the snake hiding in the form of a harmless rope. She would want to kiss him but only release poison. Her nectar was poison for him.

Who was having this pain? Who was experiencing it? He was wondering. Was his physical body? That was the suffering body. It was the part of his subtle body which was experiencing pain.

The same situation he walked away from, his suffering body was pulling his physical body right there, in that hell, in that ditch.

He was showing good, hiding bad. As showing his bad face would hurt his identity, his image. He wanted it cleaned. That was he living for, the name, the ego.

But shit was flying everywhere. It was coming and sticking on his clean ego. He was seeking heaven, where shit wouldn't be flying. He would be away from it.

His happiness was for a fraction of a second. Very small, the smallest fraction of the time he could experience. After that there was pain. The nightmare, the hell, that was painful.

7

The pain was created by the pleasure. The reality showed him the complete opposite. The pain. He realized. The only way to know the distance from the center, was to take an opposite position on the other side. To know the center he needed to experience the pain. That was how he could measure his pleasure in terms of good and bad experiences he had. And then he could find out how much he was attached to it. Every blow in the form of pain was stretching this scale.

After hearing those words, he felt the enormous blow of pain. The same pain Galileo would have experienced when only he was right. Based on his observations and calculations, he made the biggest discovery ever. He worked years to provide himself the proof that it was the Truth. The Earth orbiting the Sun. Where all the judgments, the beliefs he had based on *Shruti* and *Smriti,* he trusted his mathematical calculations. Yet, he was blamed, mocked and locked.

That was his connection to the Sun. To know that the

Earth was not the center. The Sun was the center.

Where the whole world was seeing Sun, moving around Earth. He was the pure reflection of Sun, where he felt his gravity and the duality.

The movement of Earth around Sun. The shift of perception from one point to the other point. If there were only two points present, no other point of reference, from one point it was always seeming like the other was moving. And from the other, was the duality of the observation of the movement. The perception was needed to be shifted to the third point, to determine the movement. At the center of his brain, the center at which the light coming in his two gross eyes, merging into one live experience of seeing. His whole body became still, and there he felt the perceiver. The *Dhruva.* The center of the Universe. Spinning Earth on her axis. The will of Dhruva was making Earth spin, and the will of Sun was making her rotate around him.

Now he was on the earth plane again, the plane of mortals, where he needed to act like them. He needed to act. Eat. Shit.

In the Hell, Tamas was dominant. The fight, physical abuse, mental abuse, hurting the other was the form of love. They were enjoying it, they appreciated. Where love, austerity, calmness and sweetness were being made fun of. The poison was in everyone's eyes, the devil was in everyone's eyes. If they found a saint, he became a toy for them. They knew they could abuse, beat, screw, curse but the saint would be harmless to them. The Sattva dominant saint was guilty to be in the Hell. He was holding the poison. Did not want to show the venom, did not want to hurt even the Devils, that was the Sattva Guna.

He was holding the poison received from the Devil's act. It was getting more and more venomous.

The pure Tamas was there. In the form of a female. The exact opposite of Sattva female duality. He hated that female Tamas. She was *Kali.* She was ugly. What was so powerful about her ugliness. Ugly face, no curves, full of poison. The kiss of death. Yet she was always coming back to him. A thought of her, a sight of her, would create an intense desire in him.

He wanted to be present when he was not there. He tried to remember only the good experiences and go there, but was unaware of Tamas guna rising in his absence. Now he had to face the Tamas. The equilibrium was lost, and the war was happening between Sattva and Tamas. The day and the night.

He was praised in the heaven and blamed in the hell. He discriminated. Praise was the asset, blame was the liability. He wanted assets. Not the liabilities. He wanted to separate heaven and hell and only wanted heaven. Liability was arising out of the asset. The desire to carry the asset was increasing his weight. The same source was praising and blaming. When there was praise, there was love. When there was blame, there was hate.

The measurement scale of judgment was ranging from 0 to saint on the right side and 0 to devil on the left side. From 0 to Miracles on the right side and 0 to accidents on the left side.

Karma was the cursor oscillating from positive to negative values, defining the ego based on actions performed. Those actions were the past. The past had become Earth. Solid piece of Earth. Stone. Due to his actions in the past. Due to all the actions performed collectively. He was perceiving few of them. From one point of reference. The same instance was perceived by other awareness from another point of reference. The instance was same, the perception was different. The negative scale was opposite. The mirror. The mirror was 0. The origin. Where negative was merging in positive. Should and shouldn't. Likes and dislikes. The likes to consume, the dislikes to excrete. Food and shit. The body was having their respective organs to perform those actions. What was caught in between, was him. The body, his prana was carrying. The food was taste.

The hunger was tongue's desire to taste. Bigger the hunger for taste, bigger the appetite. More intake was creating more shit.

His expression was the manifestation of the fear. His every expression was arising from the fear. He didn't want to lose. His current attachments. Current physical attachments. Those were his actions. The subtle attachments were causing his mind making his body move towards that object, to satisfy that need. The object's visual gravity was so powerful, that he saw it and he wanted. He wanted it. He wanted it to become part of him. And once it became part of him. It was attached. Now object took over him. His will. He was obeying the object. He was obeying the piece of earth. He was following the piece of earth. Wherever it was walking, dragging him. He was going with that, that was the attachment. So much attachment. As much as the thought of losing that attachment was causing the view of the hell. Which he wouldn't want to be in.

He could hear the dogs barking and see them running towards him. He was running. Faster and faster. Suddenly he collapsed. He tried to stand up. But he couldn't because as he tried to stand up, there was an extreme pain in his knees. He collapsed again. He tried to stand up again, this time, he was able to take a couple of steps, but then he collapsed again. He could hear the barking was getting louder and louder. He wished only one thing. That he could be on his feet again. The fear of getting bitten by dogs was exceeding by the fear of not being able to stand on the feet.

He jumped up in his bed, sweating. Realizing that it was a nightmare, bloody nightmare. Recurring nightmare. But this time, it was more vivid, scarier. Dogs chasing him was new but That collapsing, it happened again. It happened so many times to him before too.

The thought of being that dream, not a reality, gave him solace but next second the thought shouted, "Was that dream the reality?"

A few moments ago, that dream was as real as this waking reality. Within a fraction of a second, the reality changed.

"What if that was the reality and this waking world a dream?"

He knew that was not his imagination. That was experienced as reality. Was that He in that reality? Or Someone else? If that was him then who was now here, in that bed?

In his waking state, He was experiencing the physical world with his physical senses. When he passed to dream state, The waker was sleeping and transitioning into the dreamer. The subtle senses were same. Hear, touch, sight, taste and smell. His physical body and physical senses were inactive. Only the subtle senses were working, but he was not able to see the difference when he was dreaming, for him that time the dream became a reality. Which was real. Which was true and which was not. His waking consciousness or his dreaming consciousness. He had a dreaming body in the dream, which was not different than the physical body in the physical waking world. The appearance would have been different, but the working organs and the senses remained same. And then what happened when he entered the dreamless sleep? He did not know anything. He did not even have the awareness of his existence, it was just after he woke up he realized that as being a dreamless sleep. That was the Absence.

The happiness of being free from that horrible experience. Happiness from the knowledge that it was not real. But then there was just pain. Memory of that pain. It was stuck. The freighting vivid images were still stuck. His suffering body was stuck there. He was experiencing the hell. The knowledge of Hell. He wanted to get rid of it. He wanted to be ignorant of that. He wished it was not real. He wished it would never be real.

His fear was taking the weird form, the form of losing his loved ones, his own body. He could realize how much he was attached to his own body. Walking on the icy footpath, fear of slipping, falling, having a brain injury and may be remaining in the bed for the rest of the life. The worst form would be losing limbs. Ahhh, even just the thought was painful enough for him. Now he knew why he was waking up in this body every morning. That much he was attached to this body. This was the attachment his causal body had with his physical body.

8

The stone was vibrating. Suddenly, from nowhere. It was silent. Without any warning, it started moving on itself. The stone was aware. A sudden force. Rising from the center of the Earth, was manifesting itself in that stone. He was about to enter a Wormhole. The Shunya was there.

If he looked at that stone, he would know who was calling. He did not want to know. He did not want to hear cacophonous voices. It would hurt. The pain, the poison was attached with those voices. They were always hurting. They would always mix some poison in the form of words and the tone, which would cut him, makes him bleed for long, without any reason. The peak of the Tamas Guna, which would break his subtle skull and the Burst of energy would turn into a severe headache. The hell. Already he started getting the adrenaline gland working and releasing the poison, the acidity inside his stomach started boiling and the facial expressions completely changed as he was about to be bitten by a snake.

The Snake was creating poison only in his presence, to others he was harmless. He wouldn't bite anyone else, only him. For all others, it was a pleasure, but for him, it was a pain. Every second he knew it was Hell. But he had to face him. Snake would bite, and he had to take the poison. Snake was beautiful. Even the thought to face the snake was creating poison inside his body. He sent himself into the airplane mode. Disconnected. Disconnected from the stone. A damn piece of Earth, which was shitting. Fucking piece of shit Earth. Consuming shit of Sun.

The devil was creating hell in his heaven, through that stone. One of the huge form of Tamas guna, which would push him with such powerful force, against his will. And would leave him with wounds. The poison in words. The Snake was able to take any form. And he was always biting him. The shit of the Hell served in the Heaven.

Suddenly from nowhere, the thought of consuming some fire came to him. Why this sudden rise of desire, the hunger for the fire element, was coming to him every time. The Pranayama exercise, he had to suck the pleasure out of that fire, ringing the byproduct. Where he had no control over his mind. Where his mind was demanding poison in terms of the nectar. To hurt and to get healed. The masochist inside him, ready to face the pain. To whom he was giving the *Vish,* to whom he was offering the *Amrita.* He was sacrificing what for what. Why this exchange, this transaction was even required. With the liabilities coming in various forms. To experience the heaven, he needed to experience the hell.

Every time when his ego, his identity, was distorted by the appearance of Tamas guna, the bad, the poison, he suffered, with pain. Peaks of the intensities of the pain. He wouldn't want that experience to happen again.

The impact of that particular event, which happened years ago, was so dense, that its denseness was in the physical form in front of him. All the other elements of that event, which he could define based on his presence were gone. If he hadn't met his best friend, he wouldn't be performing the rituals. That very occurrence of the event was the seed in his timeline of the existence of that ritual. If that didn't happen, he wouldn't be aware of it ever. But then he thought, if that argument was right, that blame was right, then there was the same probability of happening his collision with his female duality in that particle collider. The impact of that event, was bigger, if he could measure in terms of time, how long he had his associations, his attachments to it.

If he could measure in terms of weight, the gravity was much larger in the later one. One in a light box, the lifeless, the full of poison, and on the other side, the living, the moving, the talking, the cooking and the loving piece of earth. Heaven and Hell. Poison and Nectar. There was no logical way to compare, these two completely unrelated aspects. But that was the argument he was receiving. That he like it more than her. He would never know her scales of measurement and sensitivity. He could have just guessed. Based on the expressions. In the form of her actions, in the form of her speech.

As he would express himself with his fingers. His expression in the form of notes was the expression of what was inside him. He plucked his guitar, and he watched his fingers. They were moving by themselves without any effort, the memory of the movement in the fingers became so physical, that now his whole awareness could transfer to the fingers and became the source of the sound. The attachment to that tune, those notes of E minor scale. Various frequencies, decreasing and increasing on the movement of his fingers. The combination of three notes was forming a chord. Just one small difference in the frequency of the third note made it major. The notes, by hearing those he was writing them. In such an amazing way the sound was transferring into the light, making it physical on the paper through dragging the pen. That was stored as a song in the notebook. Which was stored in the fingers, through repeated, learned movement. The guitar was producing nectar. He was not aware of himself anymore. He was the Note. He was the Solo. He was the Sound. That was Karma Yoga.

He wanted perfection, in everything. Those were his *Sanskara.* Which were loaded in his subconscious. He wanted to be better. Everyone around him wanted him to be the best. The first. And whenever he failed, he was punished. Physically, verbally, mentally by others. He punished himself. And worked more to make everything perfect. The perfection was ever achieving. It was always lacking. Lacking that something. Some form. Pain. The pain of not being complete. The completion was reachable only at Infinity. When he would have everything. He would be everything.

They were all seeking liberation through his perfection. Their purpose was to make him perfect. Removing the defects. Performing all the Sanskara. The perfection was perception. Different for everyone. Gold for someone was shit and shit was gold for someone. The valuation method and variables considered were different, and everyone was having their own definition of perfection. His voice was harsher and loud for someone, and some were getting cured of it. His gold was considered shit somewhere in the marketplace, where shit was getting sold at the price of gold. The downside of being Sattva was to shit gold. He would spit amrita even when he wanted to spit the poison. Even he wanted, he was not able to spit poison. But poison was there. It was coming out in other forms.

9

The nectar was not nectar for him anymore. It was not heaven anymore. It became earth plane. He was bored of the taste of nectar. Now he wanted flavors in it. He wanted to experience different taste. The bitter, the sour, the spicy. He was seeking Hell. Hell became his desire. Not aware of the pain involved. He wanted, desired. Even when his desires were fulfilled in the best possible way. He wanted more. Variations. Different. That seek was the pain. The desire was the pain. The movement of mind was the pain. The attachment was the pain. The fulfillment was the pain.

The pain was the primordial cause for the movement. The pain of being complete and lose everything. The pain at the center of Sun, he was burning himself to lose everything, the physical reaction was the light, the heat. Trillions of the colors bursting out every second.

Then on the other side, it was his male duality outside him. Having a completely different set of experiences. The weight, the gravity was becoming so powerful as they two were coming closer. Both were getting heavier and heavier. The mass was forming. The pain, of facing the opposite male duality.

The other positive. One had to assume the lost, lose of his ego. The ego was creating the speech. The pain was manifesting in the speech. And producing the physical expression of that pain in the other. No one wanted that collision to happen. They knew they both would get hurt. Yet they were facing and hurting each other.

The situations were bringing them together. One moment ago they were not aware of each other, and now suddenly they were facing each other.

The two positive poles were repelling each other. They both were feeling pain. There was a war to prove who was bigger. The bigger one would be happy, the loser would be sad. He could only experience one reality. If he was winning, he was not able to feel the other's pain. When he lost, he was the one who was experiencing the hell. The fight was for heaven and hell. Newly created heaven and hell just because of the presence of the other. Before he was the winner. Now he had to fight for it. All his plans for his near future vanished, and he was facing the uncertain. One was going to win.

The mortal was going to lose, the immortal was

going to win. The light was him, and the other was dark.

The egos were different than physical bodies. The gravity of the egos was scaling from extremity of masculinity to the extremity of femininity. Bodies were random associations of the egos, created by the surrounding and the past experiences. They were learning rules, thickening their boundaries, building the beliefs. At physical level it was body at the subtle level, it was Chitta. He was only aware of his Chitta. She was only aware of her Chitta. The difference was the layers of learning, experiences, beliefs, food, and everything which was the subject of the senses.

She had the beauty of Sattva, walk of Rajas, and fire of Tamas. She was Duality. She was Parvati, she was Seeta, she was Radha. And he wanted to give. To transfer. That drop of awareness. Inside her. The desire was rooted in *Mooladhara* and reached to *Svadhishthana,* as he saw her. That was making him move. That was making both of them move. The move was the beat.

She was different from him, his body, his intellect, his mind, his senses. But the breath was same. The smell was same. He was creating the stink, she was creating the fragrance. She was lighting fragrant candle, he was blowing stenchy *Apana.* She was cooking food, he was converting it into shit. Equilibrium of heaven and hell. He wanted to give her pleasure. He wanted to provide her heaven, but then he had to take her hell. Carry her pain. The knowledge of her pain, his presence was creating for her. Pain was transferring through speech, expressions. When she saw his pain, his movement, she was receiving pleasure. His pain was her pleasure. She was Sadist. The pain was transforming in the form of guilty. She wanted him to feel guilt. Now he was feeling guilty. He was receiving pain. The desire for pleasure was causing all those forms of pain. It was a continuous reaction. Chain of reactions of pleasure and pain. The pain was always arising without warning. The knowledge of that pain as a possibility every second, and not transforming into reality, was making him happy. He was happy not to be in the hell.

The protection was his Sattva and the dominance was his Tamas. Her caring was Sattva and tear was Tamas.

Rajas was the innate process of transformation. Sattva into Tamas and Tamas into Sattva. They were in equilibrium. Then the sudden force came. Disturbing the balance. Creating the chaos. Working as a catalyst. Movement. Energy conversion. Sound was light. Light was air. Air was water and water was earth.

That was the movement. That was the gravity.

Pulling him. The need to attach. What would it fulfill? What he would get by losing precious himself. The pleasure. The pleasure of separation from himself. The pleasure of sodium to lose its energy, giving it to chlorine and then they both could rest in peace. The pleasure within the pain.

She was experiencing the complementary, the opposite, the duality. She was his source of the movement, every movement he was making was the power of her, the gravity of her. She was Heaven. He was Hell. She had different eyes, he had different eyes. She had different ears, he had different ears. She had different past. He had different past. She was Different.

The pain was moving his body. No pain, no movement. As a thought came to his mind, it was attached. It was attached to one of the many just passing by. Mind was attached to it. It wanted it to be a reality. It wanted it to be so real, that he wanted to grasp. That was his test for reality that he could touch and feel. The mind was pulling him. Towards her. He had to obey his mind. He had to obey her. She was the boss. The sight of her was so beautiful that he wanted to be her. He wanted to come outside him in a body produced by her.

One human body out of billions available, he was only attached to her. The only human awareness, other than him in his current bubble. Inside the extension of his own body. Inside those walls. The female duality. The distance from him to center was the distance from the center to her. The inverse of his masculinity was in front of him in the physical form. There was always distance. Physical distance. But the subtle energy was connected, through the *Anahata,* through the hearts. Below it was connected to the *Manipura,* at the navel. Food. She satisfied his hunger. Choosing for him what was becoming his body. She was controlling his *Samana.* He had to obey. Only she could overpower him with her femininity. The respect. For the ability to give birth to another human. Which he was not able to. Alone. He needed her, for his desire, to reproduce.

He chose to destroy himself than her. The pain of detachment. From her, from himself. He was only defined because of her. Her appearance was presence, and her absence was Zero. The pain of Zero. Completely alone. As he was always. Infinity was separated from him. He walked away. Gave up everything, just by himself. Where Infinity was boiling at the extremes of hot and cold, it was waiting for him, to manifest. Love or hate. Happy and sad.

Sattva guna for him was becoming Tamas guna for her, and her Sattva was becoming his Tamas. The source of pleasure for her was creating his pain. And his pleasure was becoming her source of pain. Both were unaware of the reality of the other side. There was no way to be in other's position of imagination based on the ego created in mind. The other's mind could not be the subject of Samyama, he could have only judged based on the expressions through actions. And those expressions could easily fool him. How could they not? Those all his beliefs were. Fooling him. Creating the perception of reality. Making it so physical that he could touch. The sense of earth. The touch of earth. Perception of earth.

The heat inside the earth was coming in the form of speech. The volcano. He knew the strength of a seed hiding in her. He could see on her face. Causing water to come out of her from anywhere else. And the sight of it would make him cripple, where he would surrender.

The judgment of pleasure and pain was completely different. One's knowledge was ignorance for the other. The scale formed based on the past experiences. Those two different bodies had two different sets of experiences. One's pleasure was pain of other. The source of argument. The very same stimuli was causing opposite gunas to rise in each other. And becoming denser and denser. More and more physical.

Wherever there was pain, he wanted to quit. Escape. He wished to become invisible.

He never knew the pain involved in that. The solution was dark. To disappear in the puff. But his absence was causing so much pain in the presence, pain in the other, he was attached to when he was present.

10

They were running. Running inside his mind. The thoughts. Again he tried to write them down, and they were escaping. He was loving to just watch them, as he tried to write, it was creating a boundary. It was slowing down, and he did not want to slow down. He wanted to move forward because he always wanted to be in the future. He had to be in the future to secure his present. He was always living in the future. Always thinking ahead. Always planning. So he could experience the life in a better way. He thought of the present. How big or small was present? It was continuous or discontinuous? Every moment the future was converting into the past. The present was not definable for him. It could be one second, one microsecond, one plank time. Or it could be one minute, one hour, one light year. He could not find where it was starting and ending. It seemed connected, woven, in the past and in the future. He was living in the past. As he was living in the future.

He saw it at *Agya*. He knew the future. That there was pain hidden. Behind tiny pleasure. The huge pain. The pain of having the liability. Increasing his weight, getting heavy. All the assets were in the form of liability. The gravity of assets was creating the duality, liabilities. He had to pay tax and insurance in the form of worries, and he was never able to calculate the true opportunity cost of having those attachments. Revenue was running in the arteries, cost of goods sold was coming from the veins. What was in him was his blood, his checking account. The saving account, the grocery, was in the kitchen.

The moment as he rose it felt to him that he was not the same, what was he, last day, last night. That was his past. He was now there. In the present, how long he could be there, stay there. Not going in the past, but then he realized that his every moment which was happening now and would happen in the future was linked to that past. Which was also stored in the forms of feelings. With other forms. Forms of other egos. And the experiences he had with those in the past. The knowledge to satisfy his hunger was there because of his past experiences. His mind knew and took his body in the kitchen. Everything was feeling automatic. He thought that was he really doing it or it was automatic. Automatically happened every day.

The past was screaming and calling him back. Back then. Back there. The source was pulling him, back to the center. The past was the source of the present. The distance from him to the center was the radius. He was rotating around the center. There was another force which was stopping him, not letting him go towards the center, towards Zero. That complementary force was the future. He noticed that the distance twice between him and the center, his mirror image was there, the alter ego, his duality. And the circumference he would have traveled to complete one round around the center if divided by distance between him and his mirror image was always constant. The *Pi.* It was constant yet not. Its value was not having definite patterns. It was irrational. It had no repeated pattern, always getting its value more and more refined and defined with every number after the decimal, going towards perfection.

The pain was the negative scale of the feeling. As pleasure was created it had positive value, simultaneously pain was created on the negative scale. The scale of measurement was made by the data provided by his past experiences. And how impactful that particular event was. If something gave him pleasure, the desire to experience it again itself was a pain. This time, that very pain was the cause of the next move. Before it came itself, completely arbitrary natural selection of Prakriti. Now he wanted to have it happened.

His vision was the glimpse of the future. To predict based on the past experiences and historical data, defining the population, calculating the p-value, statistical limits, specifications, confidence intervals, and making an educated guess until it became so physical that he was seeing it. He wanted to touch it, so he went nearer. The imagination was becoming sight. More gravity the imagination had, the denser the sight was. The *Anahata*. Anahata was watching this. Arriving from the *Agya,* and transferring to *Vishuddha* to express in the space. Vishuddha was expressing in sound. He was hearing the sound through Vishuddha. The expression was gaining gravity from his breath, *Udana* and manifesting.

He thought that his whole future was imagined. The conclusions drawn by his intellect, based on the past experiences.

That was experience. Mind was creating the perception of time. The mind was existing in the past and future. The present was not the part of time. So the mind was always in the past and in the future. It was never there. The future was also the projection of future, not the future. Projection based on the past. The mind experienced the past. The intellect, the intelligence was present. The intelligence behind the senses, the intelligence riding on the sense perception and performing an enormous amount of calculations of right and wrong.

When he looked around himself, he started to gain the knowledge about the past. Geeta on his table. He bought that from an airport years ago. That very experience was creating a physical object, a book, in front of him now. On a subtle level, he knew that the physical book perception was generation of the light. The light falling on it and discriminating a piece of earth, from earth. His perception of sight was creating the whole experience, and his intellect was discriminating that piece of earth. There was the presence of the trees its pages were made from. That piece, every second was having the potency to be converted into the ashes if he touched it with his lighter, into a projectile if thrown at a particular speed and angle, and then, into a black hole.

If he moved that from its place, where it was on the table, the book became absent from the place where it was, that became the black hole in that frame of reference, the absence was creating the black holes. When the star was dying, its very absence was creating the black hole.

His awareness went to the book, merged with it, and

now the perception was changed, the perceiver was changed, his absence was creating the black hole, as he moved, his absence from the previous place, created a black hole there, the series of absence and presence, he was creating, when he was walking, absence and presence, 0 and 1.

He was always trying to find why he was attached. He was the master. But he needed the rope to attach that body, that awareness. Now he was attached to it. Now he became a slave. That was *Quantum Entanglement.*

One was spinning clockwise and one counter clockwise. One was perceiver, and other was perception. The perception was the measurement. Measurement of time and space. Chitta was recording it. He liked it, it was his job profile. To record. No reason. Just record. Record everything. Necessarily, unnecessarily, just record. With purpose, without purpose, just record. Without thinking, with thinking, just record. With awareness, without awareness, Just record. And then transfer. Transfer it into light and sound, into the wave and disappear. Disappear as it was never there. The Zero. All which Chitta stored was disappearing in the Zero. Chitta was always expanding, its entropy was increasing. Ever increasing. It was becoming more and more powerful. It wanted to be everything. Every thought could have ever imagined. It was storing everything. But for whom. Whom he was doing all of this work. All of this storing? He was *Intellect.* The intellect was discrimination facility. The judge. The master of the senses.

It was impossible for him to know that what happened, was destroyed. It was not there. He was making all of his judgments, all of his moves based on the knowledge of the past. That was the reason, why he appointed Chitta, so he could know more, predict better, the outcome, and have more certainty about the future. He wanted it to be good. The bad would bring the pain. Chitta had to separate. It had to have sorted, the good and the bad, the right and the left, the pleasure and the pain, the light and the dark. He wanted the first. The second was the perception of the first. He was in between. To discriminate, to judge, to decide. So he could eat the good and shit the bad. So he could throw away the garbage and keep the valuables. So he could take the big and leave the small. So he could breathe happiness and exhale the sorrow. He needed to have an experience to experience those. The desire of that experience was the pain. Pain that it was not present. Desire it to be present. The pain was creating the gravitational waves. The love was pain. The desire to feel its gravity, its presence and then just rotate around it, spinning around it. Grasp it, consume it, smell it. When it was too much, when it became too heavy, it became boring, he wanted to get rid of it, to excrete it. He had to make a hole so he could take it out. The place from where his shit was coming out. Taking all the blame. He was *Asshole.*

The part of his body became the entrance of the offerings. He had to present himself. They were coming and just wanted to insert something in him, to feed everything and anything they have. What was the pleasure they were receiving in his fulfillment? To cook the best food to feed him. They were seeking completion in his completion. He had to be nice to them, because he loved all of them, they were all his loved ones. They would be happy if he was perfect. They would be happy if he was happy. They would be sad if he was sad. What was this connection? He had to say nice things even if they were screwing the holes on each side of his skull. To act good was a virtue and to act bad was a sin. Everyone wanted to claim the good. For them, the biggest virtue, the biggest achievement was to move him. Move him according to their will. For that their will had to be different from his. If he was going north, they had to move him south. They wanted control over him. The mirage of the will. The mirage of the Ego. If he moved according to them, he was obeying. They owned him. They were masters, he was a slave. He had to do whatever they wanted.

And they were everywhere. To bug him. To ask questions. He was the solution to their problems. They knew. If he spoke than there were questions connected. A source of endless chain of questions. He wanted to keep the good and leave the bad. The desire was dragging him. To heaven and to hell.

Every time he felt after he spoke that he made a mistake. He had to keep quite. Whenever he spoke the other became powerful. He was creating ego, a boundary around himself. He needed to learn to control the desire of speaking. His majority of upset, the uncertainty could be decreased if he was quite. He could have lied if spoke, but there was no lie in silence. He was free if he was silent. If he spoke, he came in other's boundary. He was not speaking, he was not speaking. There was no need to lie, nor speak the truth. The presence of other was also creating a subtle boundary. He wanted to make the other good. He had to get crazy. Not to care about the other's words. He was in heaven. Alone. The other was hell. The other he wanted to make happy. He had to be outside, to speak, he was coming outside of him in the form of speech. He did not want to leave the body. When he was quite, the whole existence became quite. The deep sleep was the pinnacle of quietness. The deep sleep. The *Sushupti.* Had no dreams. The good, the bad, the lie, the truth was happening even in dreams. The other egos were existing in his dreams. And he was having his ego too. The Sushupti. The quietness. No vibrations. No light. No sound. What ever happened inside him only he knew. Even after his death. The depth inside him was bigger, deeper.

11

The presence of the other was creating a complete different duality, a completely different experience. The before one was now two. Without any reason, a natural selection of Prakriti. And that now became his reality, the reality he was experiencing now. The schizophrenic was telling him that this all was happening within him. But there was something else outside he could feel the presence of. Another collection of random variables and constants. An organization of various elements, a particular voice, a unique body made of the same food, exactly as his body. Yet the same food was converting in two different bodies. The same water was converting in two different human forms. The two different forms of human intelligence, the intelligence of the earth. Two pieces of the earth, alive, walking, yet separate from each other. The earth was changing forms, yet the water was same. It was changing the color, the form whenever it was coming in touch with the earth.

He could perceive, he could feel the presence outside

him. The duality of him, the duality of his human form. The female form of him, outside him. He was experiencing the reality in another human body. And he would never know what was in her mind. It could be completely deceiving. It was always deceiving. He deceived himself. Always. He judged her based on his knowledge of her expressions. How good he was at reading the expressions of the other humans and then inferring what would be in their mind. He might have always been wrong. It would have always been a lie.

The light was creating all of these experiences. Through which he could see himself, her, everything. It was all his sense perception of light, through his eyes, his mind and his intellect. The whole experience would be completely different in the absence of light. In the dark. In the dark, he was experiencing a different form of her. Then the other senses were amplifying. The touch. The touch was as beautiful as the sight. It was not possible to make a judgment which was better. When he moved his hands on her body, his perception of touch was creating an experience. How it could be a lie, that was the live experience. That was his presence. Yet it was a lie when there was light. Because now the light became the truth. Yet it could not be the truth as it was changing with his each blink. Then what would be it? Was the light truth, or dark? That was the duality.

The light was creating the dark, and dark was creating the light. Every photon, the tiny particle of light was converting into the dark as it was traveling. It was not present there where it was a moment ago.

The experience of the presence was creating the perception of time and space. Time was being divided in past and future. Space was also creating its three dimensions. He saw that what just happened was not completely gone, it was present there in its subtle form. In his memory. In the form of Chitta. That was past. The past was creating its mirror image as future. When he looked at left, it was past, when he looked at right it was future. The knowledge of the past was creating the perception of the future. The memory was thus creating the imagination. And that imagination was creating the memory again. That was his mind.

His mind wanted to grasp it, take it, merge with it, make it his, what was his not. As a child would want to put everything in his mouth, he wanted to be it, he tried to grasp what was there. The five senses came out of him, as five fingers were coming out when the child wanted to grab it. Now he could perceive in five ways. Trying to increase his grasp each and every moment. Be bigger and bigger. How big? How big he needed to be when he could grasp everything, with his five senses.

What he just experienced it felt good. He wanted to experience again. The discrimination happened, duality was created, the duality of good and bad. He defined himself. The ego defined itself. There was a boundary. There was separation. They were now two. And then there was a process of one changing into another. Thus there was an observer. An object. And a process of observation. The desire was being created because of his past experience, memory.

What could he perceive? What could he grasp? There was just wave. Appearing in smaller and smaller waves, infinite, infinite possibilities. As his awareness went through these five senses, he perceived these waves as matter. As particles, manifested form of wave, the physical manifestation was happening because of his act of perception.

That came. The drop in the form of a thought. In the subtle form and got caught at *Vishuddha.* He went outside and saw the duality. The other perception. Her perception. She was right. He was right. And still, there was an argument. The opposite poles of male female duality were repulsing each other. They only needed to be turned to attract each other. But he didn't want to move. He didn't want to turn. The gravity of the earth was not letting him turn. His ego. His ego was so powerful, it did not want to concede and was working against his will to turn. He would lose his masculinity, and the femininity would take over him. It was always there. Rising from the *Mooladhara,* from the earth. The fire of *Manipura* burned it, and it manifested. As air, as smoke. The ego lost. Masculinity lost. And he shifted over to femininity. From the masculine extremity to the feminine extremity. Total surrender. The Bhakti Yoga. Letting it happen. Only singing. The Glory. She was *Meera.*

Ready to lose. Lose everything. She was desiring to merge in her Krishna, through sound. And when she was merging in him, she was lost, and only sound was there. She was sound. Merging in the Zero. And again emerging from it. It was tough to hold that energy. It was awesome to release it and let it go. Not holding on to it. The Burst of thought took the form of the air and then disappeared, where it came from. The Zero. He was Zero again. The Bliss, the neutral, the absence. He was the Shunya. He was floating, free of gravity, free of earth. Free of her. Free of gravity of his own body and breath. Free of light and sound. He was space. He was ether. And it was ether around him. Nothing else. Pure vacuum, pure absence, everything, every perception merged into the Shunya. Though unperceived, unperceivable, the only way to measure this absence was the distance between two consequent perceivable forms of presence. Two different events in the same presence. That was time. That was the perception of time. His mind was perceiving the time. It was just perception. Perception of presence. Byproduct of the space. The movement within the space. No movement, no time. The movement was creating the perception of time. The movement was happening in the space. He was perceiving the movement. He was perceiving the wave. The act of perception was collapsing the wave into a particle. The intellect was showing him wave as a particle. Many of them. Combining in various forms and amplitude of the gunas.

But he was Zero. Not attached to the gunas. Where was no movement. Everything came to a stop. Nowhere to go. Nowhere to reach. Nothing to do. Aloneness. Pure aloneness. Away from Infinity. Only Zero was able to be alone. No negative, no positive, only Zero, Alone. No movement of Prakriti. Full control. Omniscience, omnipresence, omnipotence. No will. No intellect. Pure Zero. The epitome of his deduction. Free from Prakriti. Free of all attachments. Free of devil, free of saint. Free of sins, free of virtues. At the very center. Zero. That was always him. Everything else changed from negative Infinity to positive Infinity, but he was unchanged. Where he came from and what would be his destiny.

His physical eyes were providing him the perception of various different forms, and simultaneously his third eye was destroying the illusion and combining all forms into one cosmic form. Creation and destruction of the illusion were happening simultaneously.

The earth element of his body dissolved into the earth and became indiscriminate from the earth. His mind merged into air, the intellect merged into fire. And then he was space. Ether. Where he could take a visible form and travel at the speed of light, or just remain space and be everywhere. Each and every possible location and position. Beyond the physical dimensions. It was not going to stay long, he knew that some distraction was going to come and break his union. And bring him back to the earth plane. The plane of mortals, the Assplane oscillating between heaven and hell.

He was seeing the infinite atoms, with the possibilities of combining with each other and producing various forms. The letters were ready to form words, words to sentences and sentences to provide meaning.

There were pixels everywhere. In their off position. Every pixel was carrying the possibility of being converted into millions of variations of the colors. He was Pixel.

The pixel as one. As unity. The unity was identifying itself, thus creating the ego. The process of this experience was existence. Only existence was remaining which was existing in the nodes of experiencer and experience. The nature was experienced. The experience was knowledge. It was again existing in duality.

Manifested and unmanifested. The oscillation from unmanifested to manifested and back to the Sushupti. The manifestation process then was creating the duality of subtle and gross. At the subtle level, the absolute unity had five subtle elements. Sound, touch, sight, taste and smell. The duality created the five gross elements on the other node. Space, air, fire, water and earth. Simultaneously the duality of the gross manifested in the form of gross elements.

It was starting with the identity. The ego. Identification of himself. He was becoming aware of his own existence. At the gross and subtle level. Then the ego was creating infinite alter egos, or the one was appearing as infinite. His Awareness was assuming separate infinite subtle and gross bodies. These infinite appearances were the very infinite centers of the existence. Every atom was the center of the existence. The identification, the ego being the only separation. All the humans, animals, micro organisms all the part of the earth. Or just the whole earth. Yet the earth consciousness assuming separate bodies in the form of animals, humans and other forms of life.

Having the want of having that experience again was creating a layer of the ego, and he was losing the experience of Infinity. The layer of ego was separating him from Infinity. And that layer wanted to expand, its entropy was always increasing. It again wanted to be Infinity.

Because of the ego, the gross elements were taking the form of gross senses as ears, skin, eyes, tongue and nose. To perceive the five gross elements the gross senses in physical bodies were existing. The perception was created, the duality coexisted in the form of expression, and he was having five action organs for expression as speech, hands, feet, genitals and Asshole.

The Space. That was his home. Without that he would be unhappy, sad, he would be in hell. Everything was a union with a form. He made so many homes in this journey of infinite, how many time he was happy, he was sad, everything lost, only one remained. That was Zero. Every form destroying, only space remaining. The loss of light. The light was lost in space.

As the form was changing continuously, it could only be defined as a specific form for a period of time. After some time the form was no more. The form was changed. The coordinates were changed.

That was his *Samadhi.* In the state of Samadhi, he was then the object. The subject, the object, and the process became one. The one vibration, and then he was receiving full knowledge of that object. The knowledge was traveling at the speed of the light. And then he was just shifting it without the judgment, the intellect was *Ritumbhara.* The boundary was dissolved, and he merged into the Infinity. He was *Sahasrara.*

He moved his awareness, and the forms were destroyed. New forms were there instantaneously. The perception was getting depth and form, converting from 2D to 3D. They were moving. Their movement was creating the perception of time. Trillions and trillions of universes were created and annihilated in The every step his eye took. Whatever was happening, had happened trillions of times before. That was Gyana Yoga.

12

She was showing him all. The ego of Einstein, the ego of Shankaracharya, the ego of Krishna, the ego of Shiva. The change from ego to ego was so quick, so continuous, as the movement of electrons in the electricity. Each and every second lighting bulbs, the flawless movement of electrons was making possible to light the bulb. That was how he moving. He could also slow down the speed and manifest in the form of running fan. Also could transfer to human intellect, in the form of the name. That image could be anything, infinite possibilities, he knew that he could choose, but as Zero, he remained untouched, by the movement of Infinity. Just experiencing it. If he started choosing, it would create a boundary. The resistance. To keep traveling at that speed, he was just letting it happen, and everything around him was traveling at the speed of light. The bigger resistance was creating bigger ego, and the bigger ego was creating bigger resistance, thus bigger piece of matter, thus more gravity, thus more gravitational waves, with higher frequencies, higher wavelengths. More gravity just because of its presence, as created.

He was just watching, experiencing, what Prakriti was showing him. In her macrocosmic form she was carrying infinite universes, multiverses and in her microcosmic form, she was Atom. Way smaller and far subtler than the plank scale. She was everywhere. When she was present, she was existing in the duality. The left side and right side. Even his body was her. His mind, his intellect, his ego was her. As they all were forms, all were ever changing, taking different forms, as the clouds in the sky and then disappearing. One thing which was not changing was the presence. In her physical form, she was earth, she was sun, she was stars, she was air, she was water, and she was fire. He could experience anything he wanted. He wanted to experience Sun. He became Sun and watched Earth rotating around him. That was cosmic play. The play between Earth and Sun. He was blasting with Bliss, absolute bliss, and emitting enormous energy out of him.

He was assigning values of the gunas to words, and they were becoming alive. Different forms were getting mass, the sound was converting into the mass. They were walking, dancing, falling, shattering, fucking, crying, dismembering, dying. The water was becoming earth. The stone. The words were choosing their own amount of gravity, mass, whatever they collided first with. They were attached. The boundary was formed. It was defined. Now they had to live with the gravity. Some words became aware of themselves, their existence. They evolved. They wanted to be heavier. More weight. They were becoming rock. On the other side birds and airplanes were flying, defying the gravity. The whole gravity became concentrated at the center and converted into strong force. The whole gravity was arising from that center. Where it stayed, it was increasing the form's mass. Its weight. And making it heavier and heavier. It was falling on earth. Where some were losing gravity, and some were gaining. It was free will. Free will of every particle. For him it was determinism. Everything was getting arranged randomly and was creating an order. A set of orders. Various sets of orders. Various layers of boundaries. From air to stone to steel to light to digits. Digits were levitating. Ready to be defined. Ready to be associated with the dimensions, increasing and decreasing the size of the form. The appearance of the form, the weight of the form. The color of the form. The light was falling on them. They were choosing. How they wanted to be. How they wanted to appear.

They were absorbing and reflecting. The biggest appetite forms ate all the light falling on them and became black. Some were reflecting all as a mirror. They were White. The white was converting into billions of other colors. It was all white, taking the various forms. His awareness was converting into the gravity, and those forms were becoming alive. He was raising the dead and killing them. He was creating the sun and burning it. He was growing the moon and eating it. He was snorting the earth and excreting it. He was tasting the water and pissing it.

It was presence followed by absence. Everything which was now present would be absent. He knew as a perceiver he could not perceive the absence. Once he perceived, he was there, presence was there. The absence was non existence. Non existence of the everything which could be present. When there was presence, it was existing in time and space. Which had infinite forms. That was existence. One Prakriti showing him infinite perceptions, forms, experiences. In the non existence, there was neither him nor Prakriti. Absence of them. Pure absence.

He was now oscillating between the Anima of Zero and Mahima of Infinity. Laghima of Cloud and Garima of Osmium. Where she was available to him, all the time, in all of her forms, yet he was untouched, all wishes were fulfilled, letting her manifest, she was Prapti. She was fulfilling all his wishes, he did not ask or order. She was showing him whatever he wanted to know, she was Prakamya. She took his wish as an order. She was Ishitva. He requested, and he had. She was Vashitva. She was sound. She was *Shanti.*

She was creating the perception of time. In her presence, he was moving. When she was absent, he was movementless, changeless, numberless, weightless, formless, timeless. She was his perception of space. Without her, he was spaceless. Omnipresent. As he saw her, he was attached. And she became his reality. He wanted to grasp her, become her, consume her. He wanted to experience her with all senses. He grew action organs to make her act and act with her. Trillions of them. They were aware.

His whole awareness turned inwards, and he was seeing himself as her. He was her. All his body was her. All his senses was her. All his organs was her. His mind was her. His intellect was her. He lost himself in her. He lost everything he had. Everything was her. He was nothing. He was nowhere. He was no movement. He was no gravity. He was no energy. He was no wave. He was no particle. He was no food. He was no breath. He was no nerves. He was no blood. He was no air. He was no light. He was no water. He was no earth. He was no sound. He was no smell. He was Zero. Yet everything was for him, everything was his, she was his. She was *Maya*.

EPILOGUE

There was no sound, no silence, just absence of them. Pure absence. There was no light, no dark, just absence of them. Absence of hearing, touch, sight, taste, smell, pure absence. Absence of everything. Everything which could Infinity contain, absence of all of them. Pure absence.

No love, no hate, absence of them, pure absence. No physical body, no subtle body, no causal body, absence of them, pure absence. No observer, no object of observation, no process of observation, just absence of them, pure absence. No will, no action, no knowledge, absence of them, pure absence. It was always there. Everything else was temporary. Everything else was flash, a flash of infinity.

Beyond ether, beyond air, beyond light, beyond water, beyond earth. Just absence of them, pure absence.

The sum of all which could exist, which could have existed, which had existed, which would exist, just absence of them all, pure absence.

No pleasure, no pain, just absence of them, pure absence.

No presence of awareness, no movement of it, no wave form, no particle form. Absence of them, pure absence.

No experiencer, no experience, absence of them, pure absence. No past, no present, no future, absence of them, pure absence. No height, no width, no length, just absence of them, pure absence. No force, no gravity, no mass, no energy, no atom, just absence of them. Pure absence.

No thought, no thinker, no process of thinking, just absence of them, pure absence. No memory, no ego, no intellect, no one. Absence of them, pure absence.

No matter, no dark matter, no dark energy, absence of them. Pure absence.

No Creation, no sustaining, no destruction. Absence of them. Pure absence.

Prakriti was eternally changing forms, but he was always changeless, formless. He was *Purusha.*

When he was Infinity, the absolute was Zero. When he was Zero, the absolute was Infinity.

That was his purpose. He was dwelling there in perpetuity where *Zero Equals Infinity.*